GET HOLD OF YOUR-SELF, MAN!

WE HAVE AN *EMERGEN-CY SITUATION* HERE... WE MUST GET THESE STORES *EVACUATED* AND THE PARKING LOT *CLEARED* AT ONCE!

WE'RE GOING TO HAVE OUR HANDS FULL. THIS STORE IS FULL OF WEEK-END SHOPPERS. SOMEHOW, WE MUST REMOVE THEM FROM *HARM'S WAY* WITHOUT STARTING A *PANIC!*

OUTSIDE...

STOP!

SCREEE

WE NEED TO COMMANDEER THIS *BUS*...AND ANY OTHERS THAT ARE IN THE AREA!

YOU... YOU'RE--!

YES, SIR!

WHILE...

ATTENTION, K-MART SHOPPERS....AND EMPLOY-EES! PLEASE LOOK TO THE MAN AT THE FRONT OF THE STORE! WATCH HIM CLOSELY...CLOSELY...

GOOD, VERY GOOD! NOW, *RELAX*, ALL OF YOU -- AND *LISTEN* TO ME!

I WANT YOU ALL TO LEAVE ...QUICKLY... QUIETLY. DO NOT RUN OR PUSH!

IT'S WORKING! *MASS HYPNOSIS* IS NORMALLY NOT SO EASY.

SHOPPERS, THANK HEAVENS, TEND TO BE VERY *RECEPTIVE*.

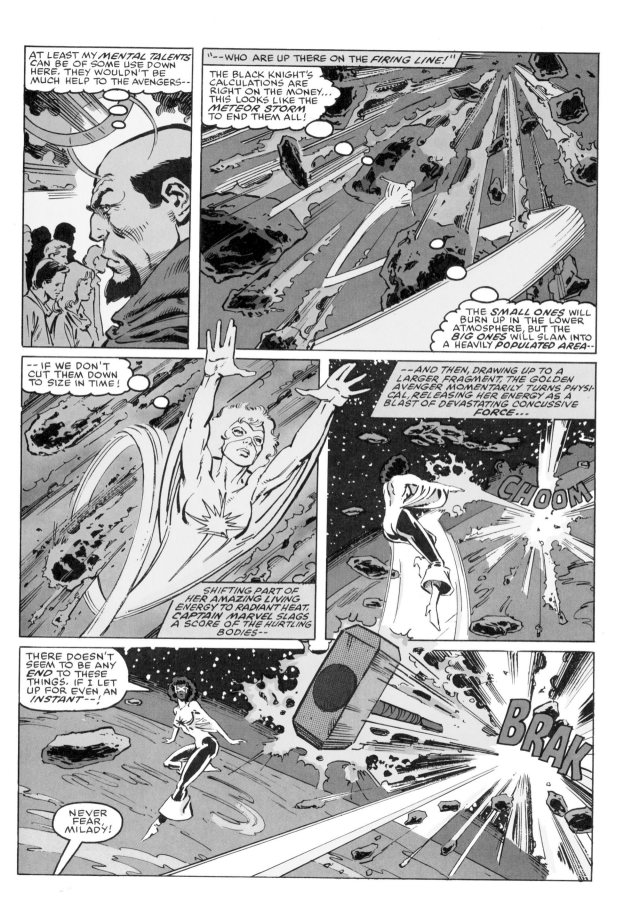

THE CALL HAS GONE OUT... AVENGERS ASSEMBLE...

...AND ONCE AGAIN, THE MIGHTY *THOR* HAS ANSWERED!

IF THESE METEORS POSE A DANGER TO THE PEOPLE OF *MIDGARD*,* THEN--BY MY HAMMER--THEY SHALL BE *NO MORE!*

*EARTH.

BARROOMM

LET THE HEAVENS RESOUND WITH THE FIRE AND FURY OF THE *STORM!*

LET THE LIGHTNING NOT CEASE UNTIL THE THUNDER GOD SAYS, "ENOW!"

JUST A FEW HUNDRED YARDS AWAY...

FROM THE WAY THAT STORM BLEW UP, THOR MUST'VE BEATEN US HERE!

NO KIDDING! LOOK ALIVE, *DANE!* BOGEYS AT 12 O'CLOCK!

CHECK, *PULSE-BLASTER* DEPLOYING...

...AND READY, *FIRE!*

BEEYOW

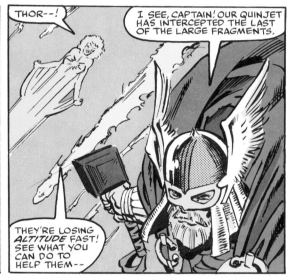

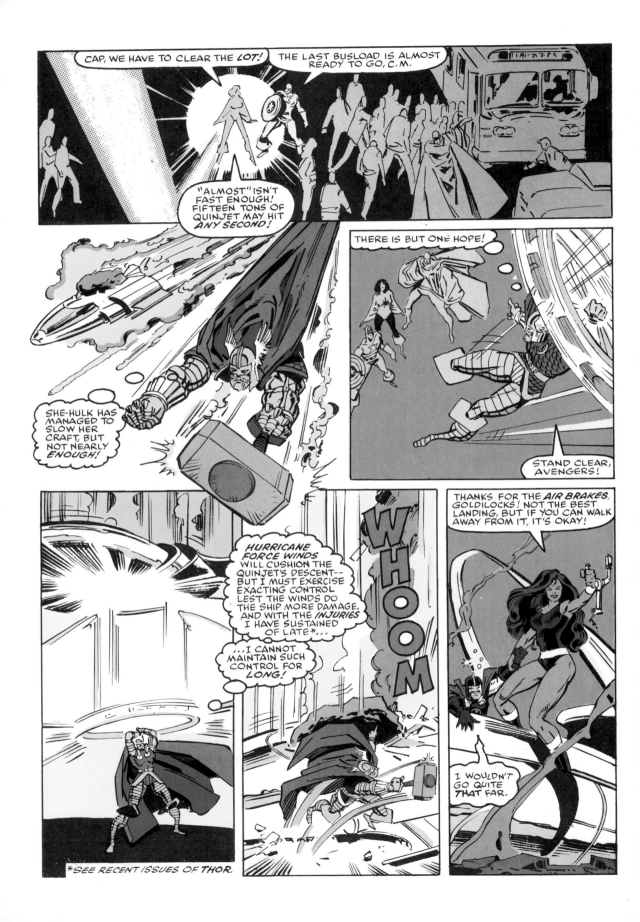

LATER... WOW! LOOKIT!

WHAT'S SHE DOIN'?

UNGH! THAT'S FUNNY...

...I SHOULD BE ABLE TO LIFT THIS EASY...BUT IT DOESN'T WANT TO BUDGE...LIKE IT'S CRAZY-GLUED TO THE QUINJET!

COME ON, YOU DIRTY--!

ALL RIGHT! FINALLY!

CAN YOU SET IT DOWN OVER HERE, JENNIFER?

SURE, PIECE OF CAKE.

WHAM

WE'LL TAKE IT FROM HERE, AVENGERS.

NATIONAL SECURITY COUNCIL! THAT ROCK'S NOW FEDERAL PROPERTY.

YOU MAY INSPECT IT FOR THE TIME BEING.

I BELIEVE YOU ALERTED WASHINGTON ABOUT THIS, CAPTAIN?

YES, THE BLACK KNIGHT DETECTED TWO LARGE ASTEROID FRAGMENTS FALLING TO EARTH...ONE THAT WOULD BREAK APART OVER A POPULATED AREA.

YOU'RE CERTAIN THE OTHER FRAGMENT, THE LARGEST ONE, WILL HIT IN KAMPUCHEA? WE'VE ALREADY ALERTED THE SOVIETS AND THE CHINESE...WE DON'T WANT TO LOOK STUPID ON THIS!

RELAX, IT SHOULD IMPACT MILES FROM ANY INHABITED AREA.

HMM... SOMETHING PECULIAR HERE.

PECULIAR? WHAT DO YOU... MEAN?

IT'S UNUSUALLY *MAGNETIC!*

WATCH!

SUCH IS THE POWER OF THE BLACK KNIGHT'S ENCHANTED *EBONY SWORD* THAT A SINGLE SWING CLEAVES A SMALL CHUNK FROM THE METEORITE. AND THEN...

W-TUKK

FTUNNG

INTERESTING.

HERE'S ANOTHER RIDDLE! THERE'S SOMETHING ON THIS SIDE THAT LOOKS LIKE *TOOLED STEEL!*

WHAT? LET ME SEE!

THEN, THIS MUST BE... YES! OH, YES! HA-HA!

YOU'VE DONE OUR NATION A GREAT SERVICE, AVENGERS! I CAN'T *WAIT* TO TELL OUR RUSSIAN FRIENDS ABOUT THIS! HAH-HAH-HA!

A FEW HOURS LATER, IN THE HEART OF THE SOVIET UNION, A GREAT RAILYARD'S AUTOMATIC SWITCHING SYSTEM SUDDENLY, CATASTROPHICALLY MAL-FUNCTIONS --

-- CAUSING ONE TRAIN TO *DERAIL,* AND SENDING ANOTHER HURTLING *TOWARD IT!*

BUT AS THE RUNAWAY TRAIN ROARS TOWARD DISASTER, A BURST OF EBON ENERGY ERUPTS IN THE RAILYARD...

...AND FROM THAT ENERGY-BURST LEAP FOUR ASTOUNDING SUPER-BEINGS KNOWN AS THE SOVIET SUPER-SOLDIERS!

<ONE SIDE, COMRADES! VANGUARD WILL SHOW YOU--> *

* TRANSLATED FROM RUSSIAN.

<--THAT HE IS MORE POWERFUL THAN ANY MERE LOCOMOTIVE!>

USING HIS HAMMER AND SICKLE AS A FOCUS, VANGUARD CALLS ON HIS EERIE MUTANT POWER TO REPEL ENERGY--

--SENDING THE TRAIN'S KINETIC ENERGY RIPPLING BACK UPON ITSELF...

...WITH LESS THAN IDEAL RESULTS.

ZZZT

<DARKSTAR! THAT GASOLINE SPILL--!>

< NOT TO FEAR, TITANIUM MAN...>

<--MY *DARKFORCE* IS MORE THAN ENOUGH TO CONTAIN AN EXPLODING TANKER!>

< YOU WERE *CARELESS*, LAYNIA! ENOUGH OF THE GAS SPILL IGNITED TO ENDANGER THESE WORKERS!>

< I'VE RESIGNED MYSELF TO SUCH SLOPPINESS FROM YOUR HEADSTRONG BROTHER....>

WHUUUF

ZAK

<...I EXPECT BETTER OF *YOU!*>

FOOOOSH

BACK ALONG THE TRACKS, THE MUTANT STRENGTH OF THE MAN-BEAR *URSA MAJOR* IS SORELY TAXED...

<THESE CARS... *MUST...* BE... RIGHTED.>

<ALLOW ME TO ASSIST.>

< ?!?>

WHILE, IN AN ISOLATED COVE ALONG THE ATLANTIC SHORE...

♪OH, WHAT A FEELIN' ...YE-EA-AH... DANCIN' ON THE CEILIN'!♪

...FIVE UNIQUE INDIVIDUALS ARE TAKING A MUCH NEEDED REST. THEY ARE MUTANTS... OUTCASTS OF SOCIETY, FEARED AND HATED BY THE WORLD AT LARGE.

THEY CALL THEMSELVES ...THE X-MEN.

LIONEL RICHIE'S MUSIC MAKES ME WANT TO SING AND DANCE THE NIGHT AWAY! DON'TCHA JUST LOVE IT, MAGNETO?

THE TUNE IS AN ENGAGING ONE, DAZZLER, BUT I PREFER THE CLASSICS.

YOU MEAN...LIKE BUDDY HOLLY?

C'MON, WOLVERINE! YOU GONNA SIT THERE LIKE A BUMP ON AN OL' LOG, OR YOU GONNA GO SWIMMIN'?

NAH. SUN FEELS GOOD, ROGUE. I'LL GET WET LATER!

THAT'S WHAT YOU THINK!

HMM?

HEY!!

KERPLASH

BZZZZ

ROGUE... DON'T DO THAT AGAIN.

I DON'T LIKE BEIN' ANNOYED ON HOLIDAY--

BZZZZ

SNIKT

ZZZZ

THIT

-- BY ANY-ONE OR ANYTHING!

JUST DOWN THE BEACH, A SIXTH MEMBER OF THIS UNLIKELY CREW TRIES TO LOSE HIMSELF... WITHOUT SUCCESS.

BOY, THIS SURE ISN'T THE X-MEN THAT CHARLES XAVIER ORGANIZED ALL THOSE YEARS AGO.

I STILL CAN'T GET OVER THE WAY THE OTHERS HAVE AC-CEPTED MAGNETO! HE WAS ONCE THE X-MEN'S GREATEST ENEMY... NOW HE'S TREATED LIKE SOME SORT OF SENIOR ADVISER!

TO THINK THAT MY BROTHER SCOTT USED TO BE GROUP LEADER--! HE'D FEEL OUT OF PLACE NOW... I FEEL OUT OF PLACE!

I WISH SCOTTIE WAS HERE... OR LORNA! LORD, I MISS HER!

NUTS, WHY DID I REJOIN THIS TEAM? WHY?!

FOR DAYS, AMBIENT COSMIC ENERGY HAS BEEN BUILDING UP IN ALEX SUMMERS' BODY. NOW, IN THIS MO-MENT OF CONFUSION AND FRUSTRATION, HE KNOWS HE MUST UNLEASH THAT AWESOME POWER!

BURROOM

WAS THAT THUNDER, *STORM?*

NO... MOST DEFINITELY NOT, IT WAS MORE OF AN EXPLOSION!

JUST *HAVOK* LETTIN' OFF A LITTLE STEAM, NOTHIN' TO WORRY ABOUT!

WHEE! TOO BAD LONGSHOT AND PSYLOCKE STAYED BEHIND. THEY'RE MISSIN' OUT ON SOME PERFECTLY MAHVELOUS SWIMMIN'!

AND SO ARE Y'ALL! COME ON IN!

YOU TALKED ME INTO IT, ROGUE! BESIDES, THE VIDEOS ARE OVER ... NOTHING ON NOW BUT THE *NEWS!*

DISASTER WAS AVERTED IN OHIO TODAY, WHEN THE *AVENGERS* ENDED A THREAT FROM SPACE ALMOST BEFORE IT BEGAN.

THOR WAS ONE OF MANY AVENGERS WHO LENT A HAND...

THOR! HE BENDS THE TEMPESTS TO HIS WILL SO EASILY.

ONCE SUCH POWER WAS *MINE.*

...ALL WERE MINE TO COMMAND. WOULD THAT MY MUTANT POWER RETURN! THEN WE MIGHT SEE WHICH OF US THE ELEMENTS BETTER OBEYED!

THE WIND, THE RAIN, THE LIGHTNING...

...AND EXPERTS AT THE AUSTRALIAN SCIENCE INSTITUTE AGREE THAT A LARGE ASTEROID FRAGMENT EXHIBITING UNUSUAL ELECTROMAGNETIC PROPERTIES MAY ALREADY HAVE IMPACTED IN SOUTHEAST ASIA.

EXTRAORDINARY! COULD IT BE--?

I HAD THOUGHT IT DESTROYED, BUT IF A *FRAGMENT* OF ANY SIZE HAS SURVIVED...*I MUST KNOW!*

SLIPPING OVER THE RIDGE, THE MASTER OF MAGNETISM HURRIES TO THE X-MEN'S CUSTOMIZED SR-71 BLACKBIRD. AND IN SECONDS...

ON-BOARD COMPUTER ANALYSIS OF TE-LEMETRY FROM THE GEOSAT ORBITAL SATELLITE SYSTEM SHOWS A BETTER THAN 95% CERTAINTY!

THE FRAGMENT WOULD MOST CERTAINLY COME DOWN IN *KAMPUCHEA.* THAT COULD MEAN *TROUBLE!* I'D BEST *NOT* INVOLVE THE X-MEN IN THIS--

--THEY WOULD ONLY DISAPPROVE OF ME LOOKING FOR SOME-THING FROM MY *CRIMINAL PAST.*

MOMENTS LATER, MAGNETO FORMS A PROTECTIVE MAGNETIC FIELD ABOUT HIMSELF AND STREAKS AWAY INTO THE EARLY EVENING SKIES...

WEEEEEEE

WHAT?!

THE BLACKBIRD'S *WARNING SIREN!* LET US GO!

WHAT'S UP, WOLVERINE?

MAYBE *TROUBLE*. BETTER PUT ON YOUR CLOTHES AND GET READY TO ROLL!

WHERE'S MAGNETO?

GONE. THAT'S THE PROBLEM.

AFTER HE LIT OUT OF HERE--

--I CHECKED AND FOUND WHAT HE'D RUN THROUGH THE COMPUTER. IT LOOKS LIKE PART OF *ASTEROID M* HAS FALLEN TO EARTH. SMART MONEY SAYS MAGNETO'S GONE TO FIND IT!

ASTEROID M? MAGGIE'S OLD *ORBITAL FORTRESS?* I THOUGHT IT'D BEEN SMASHED TO BITS! *

*BY WARLOCK COMING TO EARTH IN *NEW MUTANTS* #21.

EVIDENTLY NOT *ALL* OF IT! THE READINGS MAGNETO TOOK INDICATE A PRETTY GOOD SIZED CHUNK HAS CRASHED IN WHAT USED TO BE CAMBODIA...

...A PIECE BIG ENOUGH TO MAYBE STILL BE CARRYING SOME OF HIS *OLD EQUIPMENT.*

THAT'S REASON TO WORRY?

I THINK SO. WHEN HE OPERATED OUT OF ASTEROID M, MAGNETO WAS OUT TO RULE THE WORLD. IF HE GOT HIS HANDS ON THAT KIND OF GEAR AGAIN...

...WHO *KNOWS* WHAT HE MIGHT DO WITH IT?

SOON, AT THE AVENGERS' *HYDROBASE* HEADQUARTERS...

WHAT HAVE YOU BEEN ABLE TO LEARN, CAP?

ENOUGH TO TURN MY STOMACH, MARVEL. MY PERSONAL CONTACTS IN THE INTELLIGENCE COMMUNITY SAY THAT THE *NSC* THINKS THE FRAGMENTS WHICH FELL TO EARTH WERE PART OF AN ORBITAL BASE ONCE USED BY *MAGNETO!*

THEY'VE LET THE *CIA* SHARE THIS DISCOVERY WITH THE *KGB*... AND THEY'VE LEAKED JUST ENOUGH INFORMATION TO THE MEDIA TO DRAW MAGNETO'S ATTENTION.

THERE'S BEEN A HIGH-LEVEL DECISION IN THE KREMLIN TO *TERMINATE* MAGNETO... AND PEOPLE IN *OUR* GOVERNMENT ARE HELPING TO BAIT A *TRAP!*

YOU'RE SAYING THAT U.S. INTELLIGENCE IS PLAYING FOOTSIE WITH THE SOVIETS TO PLOT AN *ASSASSINATION?*

IT'S NOT BEYOND SOME AGENCIES, DANE.

THERE ARE FAR TOO MANY BUREAUS WHICH OPERATE *OUTSIDE* THE LAW.

THOUGH I CAN UNDERSTAND THE DESIRE TO BE RID OF A WORLD-CLASS MENACE LIKE *MAGNETO.*

MANY HAVE BEEN THE CRIMES OF MAGNETO, BUT THERE IS NO HONOR IN SUCH AN AMBUSH.

I'M AFRAID I'M WOEFULLY *IGNORANT* OF MAGNETO'S RECORD. I TAKE IT THE REST OF YOU HAVE *MET* THE MAN?

AT ONE TIME OR ANOTHER, DOCTOR, AND THEY HAVEN'T BEEN PLEAS- ANT EX- PERIENCES. MAGNETO HAS HAD QUITE AN *INFAMOUS* HISTORY...

...BEGINNING WITH HIS TAKE-OVER OF THE *CAPE CITADEL* MISSILE BASE,* NOT LONG AFTER THAT, HE OVERTHREW THE GOVERNMENT OF *SANTO MARCO*, SETTING HIMSELF UP AS ABSOLUTE RULER!**

HE DARED TRY TO AROUSE THE PEOPLE AGAINST *ME*??! TAKE HIM TO THE DUNGEON!

*X-MEN #1,
**X-MEN #4.

'TWAS NOT LONG AFTERWARDS THAT *I* FIRST ENCOUNTERED THE MISCREANT IN NEW YORK HARBOR. WHEN HE FOUND HIS POWERS SORELY TESTED BY MY STRENGTH, HE AT-TEMPTED TO SLAY ME WITH A *THERMO-NUCLEAR BOMB.**

HAD IT EXPLODED, ALL IN THE GREAT CITY WOULD HAVE PERISHED!

*JOURNEY INTO MYSTERY #109.

THAT WASN'T HIS FIRST TRY AT USING A *NUKE*, THOR.

ACCORDING TO OUR FILES, HE SET A TRAP FOR THE ORIGINAL X-MEN IN SANTO MARCO WITH A BOMB WHICH WOULD HAVE LEFT THAT NATION A WASTELAND! THOSE CRIMES SHOULD HAVE PUT HIM AWAY FOR LIFE.

THEY WOULD HAVE... IF THE WORLD COURT HADN'T DECIDED TO STRIKE ALL CHARGES ARISING FROM ACTS COMMIT-TED BEFORE MAGNETO WAS REDUCED TO INFANCY.* IN THE EYES OF THAT COURT, HE WAS "REBORN" AS A NEW MAN.

*IN DEFENDERS #16.

IT'S SHOCKING THAT ANY COURT COULD MAKE SUCH A DECISION. I SAW MAGNETO IN ACTION AFTER HIS SO-CALLED "*REBIRTH!*" HE ATTACKED ME WITHOUT PROVO-CATION...

...WANTONLY DESTROYED A RESEARCH FACILI-TY...AND ABDUCTED AND *TORTURED* ANOTHER MUTANT!*

*CAPTAIN AMERICA ANNUAL #4.

"IF THAT WASN'T EVIDENCE ENOUGH OF HIS TRUE COLORS, SOME WEEKS LATER, HE SACKED A SERIES OF AEROSPACE INSTALLATIONS IN AUSTRALIA AND NEW ZEALAND.

"AND THE *BEAST* RE-PORTED THAT MAGNETO HAD ALSO IMPRISONED THE X-MEN, AND WAS TORTURING THEM AROUND THAT TIME!"*

* THE BEAST, A FORMER X-MAN & AVENGER, WAS WITNESS IN X-MEN #112-113.

IF *THAT* STILL WASN'T ENOUGH TO CONVICT MAGNETO, WHAT HE DID TO THE RUSSIANS SHOULD HAVE BEEN!

I RECALL HEARING ABOUT THAT, DIDN'T HE WRECK A SUBMARINE?

WRECK IT? HE *SANK* ONE AT SEA, KILLING ALL ABOARD!

"AND THEN, HE USED HIS CONTROL OF MAGNETISM TO CREATE A *VOLCANO* IN THE MIDDLE OF *VARYKINO*...DESTROYING THE ENTIRE CITY!"*

*IN X-MEN #150.

AFTER THE WAY MAGNETO SKIPPED OUT ON HIS TRIAL,* I CAN SEE WHY THE SOVIETS WOULD BE OUT FOR BLOOD.

YES, THEY'RE VERY SERIOUS ABOUT THIS. MY SOURCES SAY THEIR *SUPER-SOLDIER* TEAM MAY BE ENLISTED TO GET MAGNETO.

* X-MEN #200.

SO...WHAT DO WE DO *NOW*?

I GET THE FEELING OUR SPY-BOYS WOULD RATHER WE DO NOTHING.

MAYBE WE SHOULD JUST SIT TIGHT AND LET THE *SOVIETS* TAKE HIM.

NO! THAT WOULD BE *WRONG*!

AND WITH THE WHOLE WORLD IN THE GRIP OF ANTI-MUTANT *HYSTERIA*, AN ASSASSINATION WILL MAKE THINGS *WORSE*!

I AGREE. THE WORLD WAS CHEATED OUT OF BRINGING *ADOLF HITLER* TO JUSTICE. WE *MUSTN'T* BE STOPPED FROM BRINGING MAGNETO TO TRIAL!

EVERY INDIVIDUAL DESERVES A FAIR TRIAL... HUMANITY DESERVES IT.

KAMPUCHEA...

HERE, ON THE FERTILE PLAIN SOUTH OF THE *KULEN HILLS*, THE GREAT TEMPLES OF THE ANCIENT KHMER PEOPLE SLOWLY DISINTEGRATE UNDER THE ONSLAUGHT OF NATURE AND CHANGING IDEOLOGIES.

HERE, THE WORLD'S MOST NOTORIOUS MUTANT HAS COME SEARCHING FOR SOMETHING OUT OF HIS PAST...

I'M GETTING CLOSER, I CAN FEEL THE *FIELD EFFECT* EMANATING FROM THE ASTEROID FRAGMENT...LESS THAN 50 KILOMETERS DISTANT.

A FEW MORE MINUTES AND I'LL HAVE A MORE DEFINITE *FIX.* IF I CAN AVOID ANY ROVING PATROLS OF MILITIAMEN, I SHOULD BE ABLE TO LOCATE MY TARGET BEFORE NIGHTFALL.

BUT SUDDENLY...

DON'T GO ANY FURTHER MAGNETO!

GHAH!

AND AS THE MUTANT'S BLINDING VISION CLEARS, THE BLINDING LIGHT BEFORE HIM TAKES ON *HUMAN FORM*...

ON BEHALF OF THE UNITED NATIONS, I PLACE YOU UNDER *ARREST!* SURRENDER, AND THERE WILL BE NO NEED TO USE *FORCE.*

CAPTAIN MARVEL?! YOU GIVE ME LITTLE *CHOICE*...

CHAPTER TWO: UNEASY ALLIES!

THE NEXT INSTANT, THE *CRIMSON DYNAMO* SUDDENLY FINDS...

I--IT CANNOT BE! MY ARMOR'S POWER SUPPLY IS *OVER-LOADING!*

COMPUTER SYSTEMS ARE SHUTTING DOWN... MUST LAND BEFORE I LOSE CONTROL OF MY BOOT JETS.

WHAT--? *CAPTAIN MARVEL?!*

THAT'S RIGHT, DYNAMO! I THOUGHT THAT A FEW EXTRA *MEGAVOLTS* WOULD TAKE THE WIND OUT OF YOUR SAILS!

HE'S ALL YOURS, *CAPTAIN AMERICA!*

WHILE...

ARE YOU PETRIFIED BY THE SIGHT OF *URSA MAJOR*, AVENGER?

AVENGER? WHAT IS HE TALKING ABOUT?

FIRST, MY PREY BECOMES A *PHANTASM,* AND NOW THE JUNGLE ITSELF ATTACKS ME! HAS THE WORLD GONE MAD, OR HAVE *I?*

YOU SAW WHAT I *WISHED* YOU TO SEE, MAN-BEAR... AND THOSE VINES ARE MINE TO MANIPULATE!

SUCH IS THE POWER OF *DOCTOR DRUID!*

WELL, AH'M NOT WAITIN' AROUND TO SEE WHO WINS!

LET'S HIGH-TAIL IT OUTTA HERE!

GO AHEAD. I'M STAYIN'!

WOLVERINE, NO! ROGUE HAS THE RIGHT IDEA!

THESE RUSSKIES WANT A FIGHT, STORM, THEY GOT ONE!

BUT IF THE AVENGERS DEFEAT THEM, THEY WILL FIGHT US TO RECAPTURE MAGNETO! WE MUST GO NOW!

LOOK! THE X-MEN ESCAPE WITH MAGNETO!

LET'S CALL A TRUCE, DYNAMO! HELP US BRING MAGNETO TO JUSTICE BEFORE THE WORLD COURT!

NYET! HE HAS ALREADY BEEN FOUND GUILTY OF SINKING A SUBMARINE BY A SPECIAL TRIBUNAL OF THE SUPREME SOVIET!

CAP AND THE ARMORED MAN LOOK LIKE THEY MIGHT FOLLOW US... I CAN'T LET THAT HAPPEN.

I HATE DOING THIS... THE AVENGERS WERE MY FRIENDS ONCE! BUT WE NEED TIME TO THINK.

THE JUNGLE GROWS DEATHLY STILL, AS THE DAZZLER ABSORBS ALL SOUND FROM THE SURROUNDING AREA--

--AND TRANSDUCES IT INTO PURE WHITE LIGHT...

...BLINDING IN ITS BRILLIANCE!

HUNDREDS OF YARDS AWAY...

OUR JET'S HIDDEN ONLY A COUPLE'A MILES AWAY. WE MAKE IT THERE, AND WE'RE *GONE!*

ONCE WE'RE AIRBORNE, THERE'S NO WAY THEY CAN CATCH US!

YEAH, I'LL BET OUR LI'L OL' *BLACKBIRD* CAN FLY CIRCLES 'ROUND ONE O' THE AVENGERS' *QUINJETS!* BETCHA THEY DON'T HAVE ANYTHING THAT'S HALF AS--

--FAST!

MOVING MAGNETO OUT OF HARM'S WAY IS A GOOD IDEA, ROGUE.... JUST DON'T GO *TOO FAR!*

AS SOON AS WE'VE CALMED THE SOVIETS DOWN, WE'LL BE TAKING MAGNETO BACK INTO CUSTODY-- AND MAKING SURE HE GOES TO *TRIAL!*

WE DON'T WANT TO FIGHT THE X-MEN, BUT IF WE MUST--

--WE *WILL!* A WORD TO THE WISE--!

LORDY, SHE... SHE CHANGED DIRECTIONS WITHOUT EVEN SLOWIN' DOWN!

WE COULD BE IN *BIG* TROUBLE.

HAVOK, CALM DOWN! YOUR POWER LEVELS ARE BUILDING TOO FAST! IF YOU LOSE CONTROL NOW, THE *SHOCKWAVE* WOULD RIP THE BLACK-BIRD APART!

ALL RIGHT... I'LL WATCH IT, BUT I WANT TO KNOW WHAT'S SO BLASTED *IMPORTANT* ABOUT SOME CHUNK OF ROCK!

A SECTION OF MY OLD BASE MAY BE INTACT ON THAT "CHUNK OF ROCK," AS YOU PUT IT. ANY EQUIPMENT WHICH SURVIVED IMPACT IS TOO *DANGEROUS* TO FALL INTO THE WRONG HANDS.

WHAT MAKES YOU THINK THAT *YOUR* HANDS ARE THE RIGHT ONES? BACK WHEN YOU LIVED AND WORKED ON THAT ASTEROID --

-- YOU WERE MAKIN' PLANS TO MAKE THE WORLD SAFE FOR MUTANTKIND BY TAKING IT OVER, AN' YOU WERE PERFECTLY WILLIN' TO TORTURE OR KILL ANYONE WHO STOOD IN YOUR WAY. *

*X-MEN #112-113, FOR EXAMPLE.

THOSE DAYS ARE BEHIND ME, WOLVERINE.

THE AVENGERS MUST BE AWARE OF THIS ASTEROID FRAGMENT, MAGNETO. IF IT IS ANY DANGER, *THEY* WILL DEAL WITH IT. OUR JOB IS TO GET *YOU* TO--

NO, I *INSIST* UPON FINDING IT...

...BY *MYSELF*, IF NECESSARY!

SHOULD I STOP HIM?

I DOUBT YA COULD, KID.

HE HAS MADE HIS DECISION...

...AND PLACED HIMSELF OUTSIDE OUR PROTECTION.

LET'S GO. WE'RE WASTIN' OUR TIME HERE!

FORTY KILOMETERS DISTANT, MAGNETO SUDDENLY BREAKS OUT OF THE JUNGLE AND STREAKS ACROSS *TONLE SAP*, KAMPUCHEA'S GREAT INTERIOR LAKE...

THE MAGNETIC FIELD EFFECT IS STRONGEST *HERE!*

OF COURSE! THAT EXPLAINS WHY THERE WAS NO *IMPACT CRATER* VISIBLE FROM THE AIR-- THE ASTEROID FRAGMENT MUST HAVE STRUCK NEAR THE CENTER OF THE *LAKE!*

YES, IT *IS* OUT THERE ...I CAN *FEEL* IT!

I MUST *RECLAIM* IT!

AT MAGNETO'S COMMAND, AWESOME ELECTRO-MAGNETIC FORCES SPRING TO LIFE...REACHING INTO THE DEPTHS OF THE LAKE, GRASPING AND LIFTING IN DEFIANCE OF GRAVITY ITSELF...

AND THEN...

THERE IS *MORE* HERE THAN I DARED TO HOPE... THE ENTIRE *CENTRAL CORE* OF ASTEROID M HAS SURVIVED INTACT!

MY BASE IS ONCE AGAIN *MINE!*

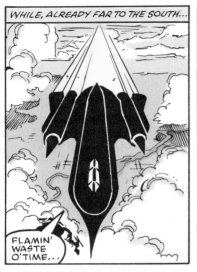

WHILE, ALREADY FAR TO THE SOUTH...

FLAMIN' WASTE O'TIME...

...RIGHT FROM THE START, WE NEVER SHOULDA GONE AFTER HIM. SHOULDA LET HIM FACE THE AVENGERS AND THE RUSSKIES ON HIS OWN!

MAGNETO IS A *MUTANT*, WOLVERINE...FOR GOOD OR ILL, HE HAS BECOME *ONE* OF US. WE OWE HIM THE BENEFIT OF THE DOUBT...AND OUR *AID*.

'SIDES, WOLVIE, WASN'T IT *YOU* WHO SAID WE SHOULD CHASE MAGGIE DOWN IN THE *FIRST PLACE?*

ALL RIGHT! ALL RIGHT! I'M JUST TICKED OFF!

KOFF KOFF

SUDDENLY, UNSEEN AND UNHEARD IN HER INTANGIBLE NEUTRINO FORM, CAPTAIN MARVEL ENTERS THE JET...

WE GAVE HIM A HAND, AND HE *SPIT* ON IT!

NO SIGN OF MAGNETO ON BOARD. WHAT'S THAT WOLVERINE SAID?

CAN'T BELIEVE HE'S GOING AFTER THAT FLAMIN' ASTEROID...AND HE CLAIMS TO HAVE PUT HIS PAST BEHIND HIM!

LOGAN, SUPPOSE THERE *IS* DANGEROUS EQUIPMENT TO BE RECOVERED?

DO *YOU* TRUST MAGNETO TO DO THE RIGHT THING?

I DON'T TRUST MUCH OF *ANY-BODY*, STORM...

...IF HE GETS OUT OF LINE, WE'LL NAIL 'IM TO THE WALL!

IF YOU DON'T, WOLVERINE--

-- WE WILL!

A SPLIT-SECOND LATER, IN THE SHADOW OF ANGKOR WAT'S ANCIENT TEMPLE...

WHAT'S THE WORD, MARVEL?

MAGNETO *SPLIT* FROM THE X-MEN. HE'S SEARCHING FOR HIS ASTEROID.

I'M GETTING A *FIX* ON HIM NOW.

READINGS POINT TO A MAJOR MAGNETIC FLUX-- 25 MILES DUE SOUTH!

THERE, WITHIN THE TWISTED CORRIDORS OF THE FORMER ORBITAL BASE...

SO MUCH HAS BEEN *DAMAGED.* SO MUCH *LOST.* BUT THE HANDFUL OF SALVAGEABLE MEMORY CHIPS AND CIRCUITS ARE PRECIOUS BEYOND COMPARE.

STILL, THERE IS MUCH WITHIN THESE RUINS THAT COULD BE USED *AGAINST* MUTANTS, AND I CANNOT TAKE *EVERYTHING* WITH ME.

THE *EXPLOSIVE CHARGES* WILL HAVE TO INSURE THAT NOTHING REMAINS FOR OTHERS TO FIND.

AFTER SURVIVING ORBITAL BREAKUP AND RE-ENTRY, IT'S A SHAME THAT ANY OF THIS MUST BE DESTROYED. BUT THERE ARE *SOME* PARTS OF MY PAST THAT ARE BEST LEFT *DEAD* AND...

...BURIED.

MY *HELMET*...

...IT SEEMS AN *ETERNITY* SINCE LAST I WORE IT.

AND THIS SUIT OF PROTECTIVE METAL MESH... I WAS THE ENEMY OF THE X-MEN, OF ALL MANKIND, WHEN I WORE THIS. MANKIND CERTAINLY HASN'T CHANGED, I WONDER...

...HAVE *I?*

I...MUST WASTE NO MORE TIME IN IDLE THOUGHT!

THE FEW THINGS I HAVE RETRIEVED FROM MY PAST MAY PROVE *USEFUL* TO ME IN THE FUTURE!

THE REST, I MUST BID *FAREWELL!*

BUT, EVEN AS MAGNETO FALLS, THE AIR IS SUDDENLY SPLIT BY THE ROAR OF TWIN RAMJET ENGINES...

÷?!?÷

THEN, AS THE CRAFT SWIFTLY SHIFTS TO VERTICAL HOVER MODE...

HEADS UP, DAHLINGS...

...THE X-MEN ARE BACK--AN' WE GOT SOME BUSINESS TO FINISH!

HEY!

WAPT

THAT *DOES* IT! YOU'VE MADE ME *MAD* NOW, ROGUE!

GOOD! AS SOON AS AH TOUCH YOU AN' ABSORB YOUR POWERS, I'LL--

HA! I KNOW BETTER THAN TO *LET* YOU DO *THAT!*

WUNK THUD!

PLOOSH

THIS IS FOOLISHNESS! NEVER SHOULDA *LET* STORM TURN US AROUND! BUT, LONG AS WE'RE *HERE...*

HIT 'EM *HARD*, KIDDIES! THE AVENGERS ARE NO PUSHOVERS!

NEITHER ARE WE!

SO QUICKLY DOES CAPTAIN MARVEL REACT--

--THAT THE OTHERS SEEM FROZEN IN PLACE.

IN AN IMPERCEPTIBLY SMALL FRACTION OF A SECOND, SHE FLASHES THROUGH THE ASTEROID'S TWISTING CORRIDOR--

--AND FINDS THE EXPLOSIVE DEVICES...

...TOO LATE!

THRAK-KOOM

BUT AS THE BLAST POUNDS INLAND, IT SUDDENLY ENCOUNTERS RESISTANCE IN THE FORM OF A THIN, HASTILY-ERECTED MAGNETIC *FORCE-SHIELD!*

MUST IGNORE THE *PAIN* IN MY JAW. MUST CONCENTRATE...

STRUGGLING MIGHTILY TO MAINTAIN HIS SHIELD--

--MAGNETO *REPELS* THE DEADLY, HURTLING DEBRIS OF THE EXPLODING ASTEROID FROM EVERYONE PRESENT...

...BUT THE ACCOMPANYING *SHOCKWAVE* SCATTERS BOTH X-MEN AND AVENGERS ALONG THE SHORE LIKE A CHILD'S DISCARDED TOYS.

THE AVENGERS' CONFUSION WILL NOT LAST LONG...

"...WE MUST FLEE BEFORE THEY CAN GATHER THEIR *WITS.*"

I NEED *HELP* HERE! THE BLAST KNOCKED CAP OUT!

RIGHT WITH YOU, C.M!

THE X-MEN'S CRAFT IS ALREADY GONE FROM SIGHT!

WHERE'S *DOCTOR DRUID?* HEY, YOU DON'T SUPPOSE--?

IN RESPONSE TO A DESPERATE CYBERNETIC COMMAND, AN ALL-BUT-INVISIBLE BEAM OF *ENERGY* SIZZLES SKYWARD...

ZEK

...FROM THE JUNGLE FAR BELOW.

*TITANIUM MAN, WHAT--?**

<JUST A FUTILE ATTEMPT TO DOWN OUR QUARRY, COMRADES. MY ARMOR HAD BARELY POWER ENOUGH TO CLIP THEIR JET!>

* TRANSLATED FROM RUSSIAN.

<DARKSTAR, YOU MUST RELEASE US!>

<SHE DOES NOT LISTEN TO HER BROTHER, *URSA*. WHY SHOULD SHE LISTEN TO YOU?>

<THE *DYNAMO* IS RIGHT, URSA. LAYNIA'S TRANCE HOLDS HER AS MUCH A CAPTIVE, AS HER *DARK-FORCE* HOLDS US!>

<I, HOWEVER, AM NOT A CAPTIVE OF THIS *ARMOR!* WORDS ALONE MAY NOT FREE HER...>

<...BUT PERHAPS A MORE *PHYSICAL* APPEAL CAN!>

<LAYNIA! YOU MUST AWAKEN! YOU HAVE BEEN DECEIVED!>

<UHN? G-GREMLIN?>

AS DARKSTAR ROUSES FROM HER STUPOR, THE EERIE OTHER-DIMENSIONAL FORCE -- WITH WHICH SHE'D BOUND THE OTHER *SOVIET SUPER-SOLDIERS* -- ABRUPTLY CEASES TO BE!

WHU--!

<WHERE ARE THE AVENGERS? THE X-MEN? WHAT IS GOING ON?>

‹YOU DO NOT REMEMBER IMPRISONING US, MY SISTER?›

‹I DID *WHAT?!*›

‹NO.... I CANNOT RECALL ANYTHING!›

‹IT WAS NOT YOUR FAULT, LAYNIA...›

"...THE AMERICAN AVENGER, *DOCTOR DRUID* DID... SOMETHING...TO YOUR PERCEPTIONS, MADE YOU SEE US AS YOUR ENEMY!"*

*LAST ISSUE.

‹OH, NICOLAI!›

‹I SWEAR THE AVENGERS SHALL PAY FOR THIS INDIGNITY!›

‹IT WAS NOT BAD ENOUGH THAT THEY REFUSED TO TURN THE FUGITIVE MAGNETO OVER TO US...›

‹THE AVENGERS HAVE MUCH TO ANSWER FOR, *VANGUARD!*›

‹...NO, THEY *ATTACKED* US*— AND ALLOWED THE ACCURSED X-MEN TO SPIRIT MAGNETO AWAY!›

*A SOMEWHAT PREJUDICED VIEW OF ISSUES #1 & #2.

‹WE MUST APPREHEND THOSE OUTLAWS....AND EXPOSE THE AVENGERS FOR THE CRAVEN *MUTANT LOVERS* THAT THEY ARE!›

‹*DYNAMO... WE* ARE MUTANTS, AS WELL!›

‹YOU HAVE SOMETHING AGAINST MUTANTS?›

‹N-NO, URSA, NOT AT ALL. I...›

‹...I MERELY MEANT THAT THE AVENGERS AIDED THE KIND OF *OUTLAW SCUM* WHO ARE RESPONSIBLE FOR THE WORLD-WIDE *ANTI-MUTANT MADNESS* ...OF WHICH WE ALL ARE VICTIMS!›

I HAVE HIDDEN MYSELF ABOARD THE X-MEN'S JET. OUR CURRENT LOCATION IS APPROXI...ARRHH!

DOC!

DRUID, WHAT'S WRONG?!

I *THOUGHT* SOMETHING STRANGE WAS GOING ON BACK HERE! WHAT HAVE YOU BEEN *UP* TO, DRUID?

-UNGH- YOU CANNOT MAKE ME *TALK*, MAGNETO!

THERE IS NO NEED FOR *YOU* TO TALK, AVENGER!

ROGUE, IF YOU PLEASE--?

HOLD STILL, SUGAR, THIS WON'T HURT A *BIT*!

INSTANTLY, THE YOUNG MUTANT'S BIZARRE ABSORPTION POWERS DRAIN DRUID OF HIS THOUGHTS, HIS POWERS, HIS VERY CONSCIOUSNESS...

MY...*MIND*!

ROGUE! ARE YOU ALL RIGHT?

WHAT AN ABSURD QUESTION...I'VE NEVER BEEN BETTER! WE'VE NOTHING TO FEAR FROM ANTHONY DRUID. WE INTERRUPTED HIS TELEPATHIC CONTACT WITH THE AVENGERS BEFORE HE COULD REVEAL OUR LOCATION.

THE CHANGE... WHEN SHE ABSORBS ANOTHER'S PERSONA ....IS *UNNERVING*.

YOUR *PSYCHIC SHIELDS* ARE QUITE STRONG, MAGNETO... DID YOU KNOW THAT?

WE HAVE MUCH MORE IMMEDIATE WORRIES THAN DRUID! WE HAVE SUSTAINED SOME SORT OF *TAIL DAMAGE*...AND IT IS RAPIDLY GETTING *WORSE!* AVIONICS ARE SHUTTING DOWN, AND THE BACKUPS AREN'T RESPONDING!

WE HAVE PERHAPS A MINUTE BEFORE WE HIT THE WATER ...*HARD!*

IN AN OLDER SECTION OF THE CITY...

I HAVE A FEW *CONTACTS* IN THIS PART OF THE WORLD. PERHAPS THEY CAN HELP ME FIND THE X-MEN.

I WOULD DEARLY LOVE TO BE THE ONE WHO *UNCOVERED* THEM.

MERE BLOCKS AWAY...

SEARCHING SINGAPORE IS A CHALLENGE EVEN FOR *MY* SPEED... SO MANY PLACES TO HIDE.

WHILE...

EVEN IN STREET CLOTHES, MOST OF THE X-MEN WILL STAND OUT IN A CROWD... SOME OF THEM EVEN MORE THAN *I* DO.

SOONER OR LATER, WE'LL FLUSH THEM OUT!

‹*DARKSTAR* REPORTING ...CAPTAIN AMERICA SPOTTED IN SECTOR FIVE. STILL NO RE-PORTS OF X-MEN.›

ELSEWHERE...

THAT AMERICAN...COULD HE BE THE X-MAN *HAVOK?*

I SAW HIM ONLY BRIEFLY BEFORE...AND HE WAS IN *COSTUME* THEN...

...BUT HIS MASK CONCEALED LITTLE OF HIS *FACE.* I WOULD *SWEAR* IT IS HE!

EXCUSE ME, I SEEM TO HAVE GOTTEN TURNED AROUND. I WAS SUPPOSED TO MEET SOMEONE...

I MUST MAKE CERTAIN...

LOOKIN' FOR SOMEBODY, BUB?

I'D KNOW YOUR SCENT ANYWHERE, YOU'RE ONE O' THOSE RUSSKIES!

AND YOU CAN ONLY BE THE OUTLAW WOLVERINE! THERE COULD NOT BE TWO MEN WITH SO COARSE A VOICE!

HR-R-RIP

LOGAN? WHAT--?

NOTHIN' TO WORRY ABOUT, COLLEGE BOY!

SNIKT SNIKT

YOU THINK TO FRIGHTEN ME WITH YOUR MUCH VAUNTED ADAMANTIUM CLAWS?

HAH! I LAUGH AT YOU!

NO ONE TOUCHES THE VANGUARD AGAINST HIS WISHES!

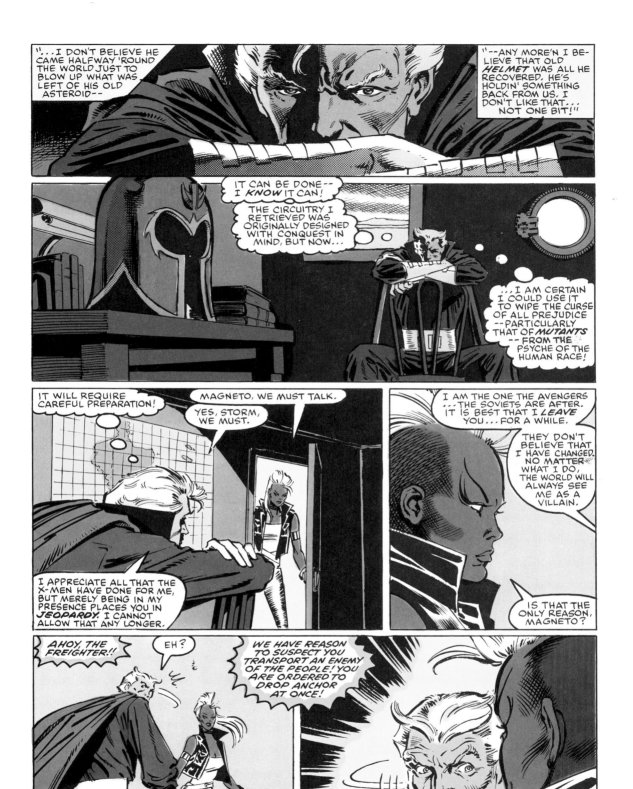

DIDN'T REALIZE...SHE WAS FLYING...SO *FAST!* WASN'T BRACED FOR SUCH A *RECOIL!*

<NICOLAI! WHAT--?>

<I WILL... BE FINE, MIKHAIL.>

WHILE, CLAMBERING UP THE SHIP'S PORT SIDE...

OKAY, RUSSKIES... THIS IS *WAR!*

SEND OUT A *DISTRESS CALL...* ALL CHANNELS... ON THE DOUBLE!

AYE, SIR!

DYNAMO! HAVE A CARE HOW YOU USE YOUR *ELECTRICAL BLASTS!* THERE ARE INNOCENTS ABOARD!

NO ONE WHO SHELTERS MAGNETO IS INNOCENT!

GOIN' SOME-WHERE, BUB?

NOT IF *I* HAVE ANYTHING TO SAY 'BOUT IT!

AT THAT MOMENT, IN ANSWER TO THE DISTRESS CALL...

HERE TRULY IS A NEED FOR OUR MIGHT!

DO WHAT YOU CAN FOR THE CREW... I'LL SEE TO THE DAMAGE!

SLICING BENEATH THE WAVES, CAPTAIN MARVEL FINDS...

WHAT A MESS! IF I SHIFT MY ENERGY TO HEAT, I CAN SLAG SOME OF THE WRECKAGE INTO A CRUDE PATCH--

--BUT THERE'S SO LITTLE TO WORK WITH! NO WAY OF KNOWING HOW WELL IT'LL HOLD...IF AT ALL!

WHILE, AMIDSHIPS...

SKKRRITT

WOLVERINE!

KLUNK

THIS IS NO TIME FOR FIGHTING, MISTER. LIVES ARE IN JEOPARDY!

TELL ME ABOUT IT! FLAMIN' SHIP'S SINKING!

WHILE, IN A LOWER SECTION...

JUST ONE MORE, HAVOK, AND THEN WE'RE OUTTA HERE!

≥HUWAUGH! HELP...ME...

LOOKS LIKE I SPOKE *TOO SOON!*

≥KAFF-KAFF≥

C'MERE, HAIRY! EASY DOES IT!

YOU...ARE HELPING *ME?*

LOOKS LIKE IT, THOUGH I DOUBT I COULD DO MUCH GOOD...

...IF SHE-HULK WEREN'T PROVIDING MOST OF THE *LIFT!*

HEY, WHAT'S THE *HANG-UP?*

OH, GREAT! THIS *FURBALL* IS TOO DARNED *BIG* TO FIT THROUGH THE HATCH!

WE'LL HAVE TO *WIDEN* IT!

THAT...IS NOT NECESSARY. ALLOW ME BUT A MOMENT... AND I WILL RE-SUME *HUMAN* FORM!

WHY DIDN'T YOU DO THAT BEFORE--?

I AM... *VULNERABLE* ...THIS WAY.

NO KIDDING.

IN MINUTES, THERE IS BUT A HANDFUL LEFT TO SAVE...

NO NEED TO *CROWD*, COMRADES -- THERE IS ROOM ENOUGH FOR ALL!

AS THE FREIGHTER'S STARBOARD SIDE SINKS BENEATH THE WAVES, THE *AVENGERS* QUINJET HOVERS PROTECTIVELY...MAKING CERTAIN THAT ALL *LIFEBOATS* ESCAPE THE PULL OF THE DYING VESSEL!

AND THEN...

VOOP VOO·VOO· VOOP

AHOY, ALL BOATS! PREPARE FOR *PICK UP!*

MY MEN AND I OWE YOU A GREAT DEAL, CAPTAIN.

ALL *HANDS* HAVE BEEN ACCOUNTED FOR...I DON'T KNOW ABOUT OUR *PASSENGERS.*

NONE BE MISSING, SAVE FOR MAGNETO AND THE CRIMSON DYNAMO?

NONE. BUT MAGNETO HAD LEFT THE SHIP *LONG BEFORE.*

THE DYNAMO HAD POWER ENOUGH TO SURVIVE THE EXPLOSION...OR TO *CAUSE* IT.

SUDDENLY... COMRADES! THANK THE STARS, YOU ARE SAFE!

WHEN THE ENGINES EXPLODED ON ME, I FEARED YOU MIGHT--!

DARKSTAR, WHAT--?

WE HAVE *QUESTIONS* FOR YOU, DIMITRI BUKHARIN!

SHORTLY...

SO...YOU *WERE* RESPONSIBLE!

WE JOINED WITH YOU TO CAPTURE ONE WHO HAD SLAIN SOVIET SAILORS,* DYNAMO... NOT TO ENDANGER MORE SEAMEN!

MANY WOULD HAVE *DIED* HERE TODAY--

*IN *X-MEN* #150.

--HAD IT NOT BEEN FOR THE AVENGERS AND THE X-MEN! YES, THE *X-MEN!* WE MUST HAVE BEEN *MAD* TO LET YOU TURN US AGAINST OUR *FELLOW MUTANTS!*

HOW CAN YOU FEEL KINSHIP TO THOSE... *OUTLAWS?*

YOU LISTEN TO *ME*, DYNAMO! YOU WRECKED THAT VESSEL WITH NO REGARD TO THE INNOCENT LIVES ABOARD...IF NOT FOR *US*, YOU'D HAVE COMMITTED THE *SAME CRIME* MAGNETO PERPETRATED AGAINST *YOUR* PEOPLE!

CAPTAIN... *PLEASE*...

...ALLOW *US* TO TURN THE DYNAMO OVER TO MARITIME AUTHORITIES.

YES, WE MUST DO SOMETHING TO ATONE FOR OUR PART IN THIS SHAMEFUL ACT.

WE WILL LET YOU DEAL WITH MAGNETO *YOUR* WAY.

MILES AWAY...

QUITE A SIGHT THERE ON THE HORIZON, ISN'T IT?

YES,... QUITE.

IS THAT A *FREIGHTER* THAT'S SINKING?

YES, SIR. STRANGE, THE WAY IT HAPPENED... SOMEHOW HER ENGINES BLEW UP.

I SEE.

WERE THERE MANY *CASUALTIES*?

THERE'S THE LUCK, SIR,... NOT A ONE! EVIDENTLY THE FAMOUS *AVENGERS* WERE IN THE AREA... SAVED EVERYONE ON BOARD!

AH. THAT IS GOOD.

PARDON ME FOR STARING, SIR, BUT I DON'T RECALL SEEING YOU BEFORE ON THIS CRUISE.

I'VE KEPT TO MY CABIN.

WILL WE BE MAKING *PORT* SOON?

YES, SIR, WITHIN THE HOUR. BIT OF BUSINESS IN *SINGAPORE*?

YES, UNFINISHED BUSINESS.

OFFICIAL SOURCES IN THE *MINISTRY OF PUBLIC DEFENSE* HAVE CONFIRMED REPORTS THAT MAGNETO IS BEING HELD RESPONSIBLE FOR THE RECENT DESTRUCTION OF A DUTCH FREIGHTER IN THE CHINA SEA! *

*SEE LAST ISSUE!

NO LIVES WERE LOST, HOWEVER, THANKS TO THE TIMELY ARRIVAL OF THE AVENGERS!

I REALLY MUST SALUTE YOUR *PUBLIC RELATIONS* STAFF, MINISTER...

...FOR THE WAY THEY'VE MANAGED TO PLASTER MAGNETO'S FACE ALL OVER THE NEWS WITHOUT LEAKING *ANY* CLASSIFIED INFORMATION!

MR. RONALDS, IT IS OUR DISTINCT *PLEASURE* TO AID YOU IN YOUR EFFORTS TO CAPTURE THIS MUTANT--

W-WHAT THE--?!

S-SORRY, SIR! WE COULDN'T KEEP THEM *OUT!*

AT EASE, SOLDIER! WE JUST WANT TO TALK TO YOUR BOSS!

HOW *DARE* YOU BARGE IN HERE?

MR. RONALDS, WE HEAR THAT YOU'VE BEEN PLACED IN CHARGE OF THE INTER-NATIONAL UNIT THAT'S BEEN GIVEN *JURISDICTION* OVER MAGNETO... AND WE'D LIKE SOME *INFORMATION!*

WE UNDERSTAND THE NEED FOR A SECURITY LID ON THE FACT THAT THE *ASTEROID* WHICH RECENTLY CRASHED INTO KAMPUCHEA WAS REALLY AN OLD *ORBITAL BASE* ONCE USED BY *MAGNETO*--*

--BUT, WE'D STILL LIKE TO KNOW WHAT HAPPENED TO THE *SOVIET SUPER-SOLDIERS* AND THE *X-MEN* AFTER WE HELPED RESCUE THEM BOTH FROM THAT SINKING FREIGHTER!

THE *SOVIETS* HAVE RETURNED TO THEIR *HOMELAND!* AS FOR THE *X-MEN*...

*AS SHOWN IN THE VERY FIRST ISSUE OF THIS LIMITED SERIES!

"...THEY'RE MUTANTS-- FRIENDS OF MAGNETO-- AND THEY'RE CURRENTLY BEING HELD IN *PRO-TECTIVE CUSTODY*...

"...UNTIL WE CAN DETERMINE WHICH CHARGES, IF ANY, SHOULD BE FILED AGAINST THEM!"

FOOL! YOU CAN ONLY HOLD THE X-MEN FOR AS LONG AS THEY *CONSENT* TO BE HELD!

BRRING

YES--? *AT LAST!* MAGNETO'S BEEN SPOTTED!

WHERE *IS* HE?

THAT'S NONE OF YOUR BUSINESS, HERO!

YOU COSTUMED CLOWNS HAVE ALREADY BLOWN YOUR CHANCE AT HIM!

"MY PEOPLE ARE PERFECTLY CAPABLE OF NEUTRALIZING HIM WITHOUT YOUR HELP!"

WHAT AM I TO DO?

I AM ALONE... *HUNTED*...IN A FOREIGN LAND... WITH NEITHER FRIENDS, NOR FUNDS.

AND, YET, I COULD RECTIFY THAT ALL WITHIN AN INSTANT...

...IF I ONLY DARED EMPLOY THE CIRCUITRY WHICH I SECRETLY *RESCUED* FROM MY *FALLEN* SATELLITE!

THAT'S *HIM!*

LET'S WAIT UNTIL HE MOVES AWAY FROM THE *CROWD!*

BUT, THEN, FATE TAKES AN UNEXPECTED HAND AS...

WATCH IT, BUDDY!

WHY DON'T YA LOOK WHERE YA--

HEY! I KNOW YOU! YOU'RE THAT FREAK WHO WAS ON THE NEWS!

THE MUTIE!!

THAT STUPID TOURIST HAS RUINED EVERYTHING!

TAKE HIM! NOW!!

ASSASSINS SPRINGING AROUND ME!

GET HIM! SOMEBODY STOP THAT LOUSY MUTIE BEFORE HE KILLS US ALL!

YOU HAVE DONE WELL, *LEIKO!* YOU LED US RIGHT TO HIM!

HE WAS EASY TO FIND, *CRAWLER!* HIS AURA IS SO POWER-FUL!

COME ON, MAGNETO! THERE'S NO TIME TO DELAY!

WHO ARE YOU PEOPLE?

WE ARE MUTANTS... LIKE YOURSELF... AND WE'VE BEEN SENT TO HELP YOU!

GO WITH LEIKO AND CRAWLER! *NOW!!* THEY'LL LEAD YOU TO SAFETY!

I'LL DIS-TRACT YOUR PURSUERS!

THE GROUND--!! IT'S SUDDENLY BECOME AS SLIPPERY AS GLASS!

C-CAN'T STAND!

HURRY! SLIDER'S CONTROL OVER FRICTION WON'T STOP THOSE HUMANS FOR LONG!

DO I DARE TRUST THESE PEOPLE?

AND, IF SO, DO I HAVE THE RIGHT TO ENDANGER THEIR LIVES BY ALLOWING THEM TO *AID* ME?

MAGNETO, ARE YOU *COMING?*

YES!

SOMETIME LATER...

WELCOME TO THE *GALLERIA*, MAGNETO!

"WELCOME TO OUR HUMBLE HOME!"

WHY HAVE I BEEN BROUGHT HERE? WHO ARE THESE PEOPLE?

THEIR EYES BURN WITH FEAR AND HATRED!

GOOD EVENING, MY FRIEND! I AM KNOWN AS THE *LIGHT!*

I AM A MUTANT WITH THE ANNOYING ABILITY TO KNOW WHENEVER ANYONE SPEAKS *THE TRUTH* -- AN ABILITY WHICH HAS HELPED ME EARN A SMALL *FORTUNE* IN THE BUSINESS WORLD!

I HAVE BUT ONE QUESTION...

WHO ARE YOU?

HAVE I STUMBLED INTO A TRAP? WILL MY OWN WORDS CONDEMN ME?

I AM CALLED MANY NAMES... FEW OF THEM FIT FOR POLITE CONVERSATION! BUT, I AM KNOWN THE WORLD OVER AS --

-- *MAGNETO*, THE MUTANT MASTER OF MAGNETISM!

REJOICE, MY PEOPLE! HE'S TELLING THE TRUTH!

HE REALLY IS *MAGNETO!*

HAIL TO THE GLORIOUS ONE!

THE PROTECTOR OF THE PEOPLE!

THE CHAMPION OF MUTANTKIND!

W-WHAT IS ALL THIS--?!

YOU ARE THE UNCROWNED *KING* OF MUTANTS EVERYWHERE, AND WE ARE YOUR HUMBLE *SERVANTS!*

LEIKO CAN EMPATHICALLY *SENSE* OTHER MUTANTS, SO WE SENT HER AND THE OTHERS OUT TO FIND YOU AS SOON AS WE LEARNED THAT YOU WERE IN SINGAPORE!

BUT, *WHY?*

TO AID YOU IN YOUR WAR AGAINST HUMANITY!

MANKIND HAS OP-PRESSED OUR PEOPLE LONG ENOUGH! IT'S TIME WE STRUCK BACK!

THE *LIGHT* SOUNDS SO MUCH LIKE I DID... BEFORE I TURNED AWAY FROM MY DREAMS OF CONQUEST!

I NO LONGER BELIEVE THAT *WAR* IS THE ANSWER, MY FRIEND! HUMANS AND MUTANTS *MUST* LEARN TO LIVE TOGETHER *PEACEFULLY!*

DON'T BE RIDICULOUS, MAGNETO! THAT'S LIKE TRYING TO TEACH A *GORILLA* HOW TO FLY!

IT ONLY WASTES YOUR TIME AND, ANNOYS THE--

--GORILLA?!

BWOOM!

AT LAST! WE'VE FINALLY FOUND MAGNETO!

LOOK! HE'S HOLED UP WITH A WHOLE HORDE OF MUTIES!

HIT 'EM HARD!

DON'T GIVE THEM A *CHANCE* TO USE THEIR WEIRD POWERS AGAINST US!

BDAM!

URKKK!

MEANWHILE...

I'M GETTING REAL *TIRED* OF STARING AT THESE--

--IRON WALLS!

AS ARE WE ALL, *ROGUE!*

WHAT'S THE DRILL, STORM?

WE HAVE BIDED OUR TIME, WAITING FOR THE LOCAL AUTHORITIES TO FORMALLY *ARREST* US, OR SET US FREE!

SO FAR, THEY HAVE BEEN *CONTENT* TO LET US ROT!

WE HAVE BEEN PATIENT LONG ENOUGH, *WOLVERINE!*

RIGHT!

SNIKT

SKRITT

HI, CHUCKLES!

IT'S TIME TO *PAR-TAY!*

PWANGG!

NOT BAD! DAZZLER'S LIGHT BLAST MANAGED TO FOCUS ALL THE ATTENTION TOPSIDE, WHILE I TAKE THE REAR EXIT!

TAA-TAA, FELLAS! IT'S BEEN REAL!

TH-THEY ESCAPED SO EASILY! THEY COULD HAVE DONE IT WHENEVER THEY WISHED!

MINUTES LATER...

I'M SORRY WE EVER GOT INVOLVED IN THIS ANTI-MUTANT WITCH HUNT FOR MAGNETO!

THE MAN'S A MASS MURDERER, SHE-HULK! WE OWE IT TO THE WORLD TO DO EVERYTHING IN OUR POWER TO HELP BRING HIM TO TRIAL!

BUT, ONLY IF IT'S A FAIR TRIAL!

SUDDENLY...

THE X-MEN HAVE ESCAPED! PROBABLY TO RENDEZVOUS WITH MAGNETO!

WHAT ARE YOU WAITING FOR? GET AFTER THEM!

SLOW DOWN, MR. RONALDS! YOU HAVE NO AUTHORITY OVER US! WE MAY BE SANCTIONED BY THE U.S. GOVERNMENT, BUT WE DON'T WORK FOR IT!

I CAN'T BELIEVE MY EARS!

YOUR COUNTRY--AND THE WORLD--IS COUNTING ON YOU!

I NEVER THOUGHT I'D LIVE TO SEE THE DAY WHEN THE AVENGERS WOULD FAIL TO DO THEIR DUTY!

ELSEWHERE, AT THAT VERY MOMENT...

THE LIGHT ORIGINALLY BOUGHT THIS SHIP FROM THE GOVERNMENT WITH THE UNDERSTANDING THAT HE WOULD EVENTUALLY TRANSFORM IT INTO A FLOATING MUSEUM AND SHOPPING MALL...

...LUCKY FOR US, THEY DON'T REALIZE THAT HE'S BEEN USING IT AS A SECRET HOME FOR US *MUTANTS!*

YES, LUCKY...

YOU SEEM AWFULLY PRE-OCCUPIED, MAGNETO!

WHAT EXACTLY ARE YOU DOING WITH THAT HELMET?

I AM CONSTRUCTING A WEAPON, LEIKO!

PERHAPS, THE *ULTIMATE* WEAPON!

PITY THE WORLD, LITTLE ONE...

FROM *THIS* MOMENT ON, IT WILL *NEVER* BE THE SAME AGAIN!

*SEE X-MEN #200 FOR THE FULL STORY!

I MIGHT HAVE USED IT THAT WAY *ONCE*...BUT I HAVE RECENTLY *MODIFIED* IT SO THAT I CAN USE IT TO REMOVE ALL TRACES OF *PREJUDICE*-- PARTICULARLY THAT OF *MUTANTS*-- FROM THE COLLECTIVE MIND OF THE HUMAN RACE!

CHILDREN SUCH AS LEIKO COULD GROW UP IN A WORLD *FREE* OF BLIND, UNREASONING HATRED!

HEY! THAT SOUNDS GREAT!

DOES IT? IS IT *RIGHT* TO TAMPER WITH A MAN'S MIND...EVEN FOR SUCH A *NOBLE* CAUSE?

NO WAY!

THINK OF THE *LIVES* YOU'D SAVE!

THE WARS THAT WOULD BE PREVENTED!

CAPTAIN AMERICA, YOU ARE AN *HONORABLE* MAN. PERHAPS THE *MOST* HONORABLE MAN ON THE ENTIRE PLANET.

I BROUGHT YOU HERE BECAUSE I AM *UNRESOLVED*. I DON'T KNOW WHAT TO DO.

WHAT IS *YOUR* OPINION?

I'M AFRAID THAT I CAN'T MAKE THINGS ANY *EASIER* FOR YOU, MAGNETO! YOU SEE, I BELIEVE IN THE *SANCTITY* OF THE INDIVIDUAL!

A MAN SHOULD BE FREE TO MAKE UP HIS *OWN MIND*... HAVE HIS OWN THOUGHTS... EVEN IF THAT MAN IS A *BIGOT*!

DESTROY THE HELMET BEFORE IT'S TOO LATE! NO MAN WAS MEANT TO WIELD SUCH ABSOLUTE POWER!

NO! YOU *MUST* USE IT...FOR THE GOOD OF YOUR PEOPLE!

LISTEN TO *CAP!* HE'S RIGHT!

ENOUGH! I HAVE MADE MY DECISION!

I *WILL* USE THE HELMET--

THIS IS *TED KOPPEL* REPORTING FROM THE *PALAIS DE JUSTICE* IN PARIS, WHERE A SPECIAL TRIBUNAL OF THE *INTERNATIONAL COURT OF JUSTICE* HAS BEEN HASTILY CONVENED TO DECIDE THE FATE OF --

-- *MAGNETO*, THE SELF-STYLED *MUTANT MASTER OF MAGNETISM!*

"SITTING IN JUDGMENT OF THIS MAN, WHOM MANY BELIEVE IS THE GREATEST ENEMY OF HUMANITY SINCE *ADOLF HITLER* HIMSELF, WILL BE THREE DISTINGUISHED JURISTS: *ALEXANDRE GILBERT DU MOTIER* OF FRANCE, *LADY JANET GRACE SOUTHERLAND* OF ENGLAND, AND *GUSTAVE ROCH UDERZO* OF SWITZERLAND."

DU MOTIER   SOUTHERLAND   UDERZO

"EARLIER TODAY, A TENSE BUT PEACEFUL CROWD OF ONLOOKERS WATCHED AS THE *AVENGERS* ARRIVED, ESCORTING A BAND OF UNIDENTIFIED COSTUMED *MUTANTS* --

"-- WHO ARE BELIEVED TO HAVE BEEN SEEN WORKING WITH *MAGNETO*."

I DON'T GET IT, *PSYLOCKE!*

WHY ARE WE IN THE UNITED STATES WHILE THE OTHER *X-MEN* ARE IN PARIS?

STORM DIDN'T KNOW WHAT STRINGS THE AVENGERS PULLED TO ALLOW THE OTHERS TO ATTEND THE TRIAL, *LONG-SHOT*, BUT SHE WANTED US TO BE HELD IN RESERVE IN CASE OF TROUBLE.

I'M STILL NEW TO ALL THIS STUFF, AND I REALLY DON'T UNDERSTAND WHAT'S GOING ON.

I THOUGHT THE *X-MEN* WERE FORMED TO *PROTECT* THEIR OWN KIND, AND TO *DEFEND* HUMANITY FROM EVIL MUTANTS.

MAGNETO USED TO BE ONE OF THE *BAD GUYS*. HE USED TO BELIEVE THAT THE ENDS JUSTIFIED THE MEANS --

-- AND THAT THE ONLY WAY HE COULD GUARANTEE THE *SAFETY* OF MUTANTKIND WAS BY *CONQUERING* THE PLANET!

HE COMMITTED QUITE A FEW *ATROCITIES* --

"-- BEFORE HE DECIDED TO CHANGE HIS *TACTICS!*"

MY LORDS AND LADY-- MY CLIENT, THE MUTANT KNOWN AS *MAGNETO*, APPEARS IN THIS COURT FOR ONLY ONE REASON--

-- SO THAT HE CAN FILE A MOTION *OBJECTING* TO ITS JURISDICTION OVER HIM!

YOUR HONOR, THE PROSECUTION OBJECTS TO THIS ABSURD--

PLEASE BE SEATED, *SIR JASPERS.*

I WISH TO HEAR DEFENSE COUNSEL *HALLER'S* REASONING.

THANK YOU, MY LORD.

MAGNETO IS A MUTANT WHO OWES HIS ALLEGIANCE ONLY TO HIS PEOPLE, AND NOT TO ANY COUNTRY.

HE IS THE *UNIFORMED ARMED FORCE* OF MUTANTKIND!

AND, HE CLAIMS FOR HIMSELF THE SAME STATUS ANY SUCH FORCE WOULD HAVE UNDER ANY OTHER STATE OR ITS EQUIVALENT.

SINCE HIS PEOPLE HAVE NOT SIGNED THE GENEVA CONVENTIONS, HE DOES NOT FEEL BOUND BY THEM--

-- AND THAT INCLUDES THE *JURIS-DICTION* OF THIS COURT OVER HIM. HE NEITHER *CONSENTS* TO, NOR *RECOGNIZES* IT.

YOUR MOTION HAS BEEN *NOTED*, COUNSELOR--

-- AND DENIED!

SIR JASPERS, PROCEED TO YOUR FIRST WITNESS.

STATE YOUR FULL NAME, PLEASE.

I AM *ADMIRAL GREGORI MIHAILOVITCH SUVOROV.*

ADMIRAL, YOU ARE CURRENTLY THE COMMANDER-IN-CHIEF OF THE SOVIET UNION'S NUCLEAR *SUBMARINE* FORCE.

IN YOUR OWN WORDS, PLEASE TELL THE COURT WHAT HAPPENED TO THE SUBMARINE *LENINGRAD.*

THE ACCUSED SANK IT... KILLING HER ENTIRE CREW.*

*IN X-MEN #150!

ISN'T IT TRUE THAT THE *LENINGRAD* HAD FIRED ON MAGNETO?

YES... BUT ONLY *AFTER* HE HAD THREATENED TO ATTACK THE SOVIET UNION.

THANK YOU, ADMIRAL.

LET THE RECORD SHOW THAT THE *LENINGRAD* WAS ACTING IN *SELF-DEFENSE* IN RESPONSE TO MAGNETO'S AGGRESSION!

MORE WITNESSES ARE CALLED--

--AND THE COURT LEARNS THAT MAGNETO ALSO USED HIS POWERS TO CREATE A *VOLCANO* WHICH DEVASTATED THE SOVIET CITY OF *VARYKINO*--

*X-MEN #150!

--AND THAT HE DE-LIBERATELY DESTROYED AEROSPACE INSTAL-LATIONS IN *AUSTRALIA* AND *NEW ZEALAND!**

*X-MEN #112-113!

TIME AND AGAIN, GABRIELLE HALLER RAISES *OBJECTIONS* TO CERTAIN KEY TESTIMONIES, BUT THE RESULT IS ALWAYS THE SAME...

OBJECTION *DENIED!*

PLEASE PROCEED, SIR JASPERS.

MY FINAL WITNESS IS *CAPTAIN AMERICA.*

MANY PEOPLE HAVE ALREADY TESTIFIED ABOUT MAGNETO'S PAST VILLAINY, BUT HE CLAIMS THAT HE'S *REFORMED*...THAT HE'S LEARNED THE ERROR OF HIS PAST WAYS.

IN YOUR OPINION, CAPTAIN...*IS HE TELLING THE TRUTH?!*

I OBJECT, YOUR HONOR!

IF IT PLEASE THE COURT, I AM CALLING THE GOOD CAPTAIN AS AN *EXPERT WITNESS*.

HE HAS UNQUESTIONABLE EXPERIENCE IN REGARD TO SUPERHUMAN CRIMINALS IN GENERAL... AND *MAGNETO* IN PARTICULAR.

IN THIS ONE, SPECIFIC INSTANCE, I BELIEVE HIS OPINION HAS *MERIT*.

THE WITNESS MAY ANSWER THE QUESTION.

NO.

I DO NOT BELIEVE THAT MAGNETO HAS *REALLY* LEARNED THE ERROR OF HIS WAYS...

...EVEN THOUGH HE, HIMSELF, MAY *THINK* HE HAS!

THANK YOU, CAPTAIN.

THIS TRIAL IS A *FARCE!*

GABRIELLE IS DOING HER BEST, BUT I DON'T HAVE A *CHANCE!*

I NEVER DID!

THE CHIEF JUSTICE HAS BEEN PREJUDICED AGAINST ME FROM THE START! *WHY?* WHAT DOES HE HOPE TO GAIN?

DOESN'T HE *REALIZE* THAT MUTANTS ACROSS THE PLANET WILL RISE UP IN BLOODY REVOLT IF I AM CONDEMNED TO *DEATH?!*

I CAN ONLY KEEP THE *PEACE*, AND CONTINUE TO SERVE MY PEOPLE IF I AM *SET FREE!*

AND, YET, I VOWED TO *ACCEPT* THE VERDICT OF THIS COURT!

HOW CAN I *HONOR* THAT VOW KNOWING THAT SO MANY *INNOCENTS* WILL DIE BECAUSE OF IT?!

SOMETIME LATER...

IT'S ALMOST OVER...

...THE JUDGES HAVE PROMISED A VERDICT BY TOMORROW.

IT'S BEEN A FASCINATING OPPORTUNITY TO SEE *INTERNATIONAL LAW* IN ACTION. THE ISSUES ARE SO COMPLEX!

UH-OH! I SUDDENLY FEEL VERY STRANGE--!

IT'S ALMOST AS IF SOME *OUTSIDE FORCE* IS TUGGING AT ME!

MIGHT AS WELL CHECK IT OUT!

I WAS *RIGHT!* SOMEONE HAS BEEN TRYING TO COMMUNICATE WITH ME ON THE ELECTRO-MAGNETIC SPECTRUM--AND HE WANTS ME TO *MEET* HIM ACROSS TOWN!

CAPTAIN MARVEL! I MUST APOLOGIZE FOR MY ABRUPT SUMMONS, BUT I AM CERTAIN THAT YOU WILL UNDERSTAND THE NEED FOR *HASTE* ONCE I'VE EXPLAINED THE SITUATION!

WHAT'S WRONG, MAGNETO?

THE WORLD IS ON THE BRINK OF A *DEVASTATING WAR,* AND *YOU ALONE* CAN HELP AVERT IT!

YOU MUST FLY TO SINGAPORE, FIND THE GIRL-CHILD *LEIKO,* AND ARRANGE WITH HER SPONSOR--A MUTANT KNOWN AS *THE LIGHT*-- TO SEND HER HERE IMMEDIATELY.

WHY? WHAT'S HAPPENED?!

I HAVE FINALLY REALIZED WHY CHIEF JUSTICE *DU MOTIER* HAS BEEN AGAINST ME FROM THE VERY START!

HE'S SECRETLY A *MUTANT* HIMSELF-- A RADICAL--WHO MEANS TO *MARTYR* ME!

LEIKO CAN DETECT OTHER MUTANTS!

I NEED HER TO EXPOSE *DU MOTIER* BEFORE HE CAN USE MY DEATH TO SPARK AN *INSANE WAR* BETWEEN MUTANTKIND AND HUMANITY!

I THINK YOU'RE GRASPING AT *STRAWS,* MAGNETO--BUT, THE AVENGERS DID PROMISE YOU A *FAIR TRIAL*-- SO I'LL DO WHAT I CAN TO *HELP!*

CONVERTING HER BODY INTO LIVING ENERGY, *CAPTAIN MARVEL* STREAKS ACROSS THE GLOBE AT THE SPEED OF LIGHT...

...UNAWARE THAT *MAGNETO'S* CONSCIOUSNESS RIDES MAGNETICALLY ALONGSIDE...

AND, BARELY A MOMENT LATER...

THERE'S THE *SHIP* MAGNETO DESCRIBED!

I JUST HOPE HIS *FRIENDS* ARE STILL HERE!

BUT, INSIDE...

MY GOD--!

Y-YOU WERE WITH THE ONES WHO TOOK MAGNETO FROM US!

H-HE COULD HAVE *PRE-VENTED* THIS!

WHAT HAPPENED HERE? WHO DID THIS?!

C-CRAZIES! MAGNETO'S TRIAL BROUGHT THEM OUT OF HIDING! MADE THEM THINK IT'S SAFE TO HUNT--*TO KILL US!!*

BUT, WE'LL *STRIKE BACK!* I GATHERED UP MAGNETO'S OLD HELMET AND HIS DIS-CARDED CIRCUITRY AS A SYMBOL OF OUR STRENGTH-- *OUR FURY!!*

THE GIRL... LEIKO... WHERE IS SHE?

SHE WAS OUR MOST PRECIOUS *FLOWER*...OUR HOPE... OUR FUTURE...

THERE SHE *LIES*--

--AS BROKEN AND TWISTED AS ALL OUR *OTHER* DREAMS!

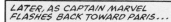

LATER, AS CAPTAIN MARVEL FLASHES BACK TOWARD PARIS...

THAT OLD MAN BEGGED ME *NOT* TO NOTIFY THE AUTHORITIES! *OTHER* MUTANTS WERE ALREADY ON THEIR WAY OVER TO TREAT THE WOUNDED, AND HE FEARED FOR *THEIR* SAFETY AS WELL!

PERHAPS I SHOULDN'T HAVE *LISTENED* TO HIM...

IT'S ONLY BEEN ABOUT TEN MINUTES SINCE I LEFT MAGNETO!

I HAVE PLENTY OF TIME FOR A SMALL *DETOUR*--

--TO LOOK IN ON CHIEF JUSTICE *DU MOTIER* WHILE I'M STILL INVISIBLE IN MY NEUTRINO FORM!

...IT WAS AN EXTREMELY DIFFICULT DECISION TO RENDER, ALEXANDRE.

INDEED, LADY SOUTHERLAND, ESPECIALLY WHEN ONE CONSIDERS THE CURRENT ANTI-MUTANT CLIMATE IN THE WORLD.

CONDEMNING MAGNETO TO DEATH COULD VERY WELL IGNITE A *WAR* BETWEEN MUTANTS AND MEN.

OF COURSE, FROM MANKIND'S POINT OF VIEW, NOW IS THE *TIME* FOR SUCH A WAR...WHEN IT COULD *WIN.*

WHO KNOWS *HOW* POWERFUL MUTANTS COULD GROW IN THE FUTURE?

TO MANKIND!

AHEM, I WOULD PREFER TO DRINK TO *JUSTICE!* YOUR WORDS SMACK OF RACISM.

MINUTES LATER...

SO *DU MOTIER* IS HUMAN! I KNEW HE WANTED WAR--BUT I TOTALLY MISINTERPRETED HIS REASONS.

AND THEY'VE DECIDED TO *CONDEMN* ME--?

NO... I COULDN'T TELL WHICH WAY THEY VOTED.

PLEASE *LEAVE* ME NOW. I MUST PREPARE MYSELF FOR TOMORROW.

BUT--

PLEASE, I WISH TO BE *ALONE*.

AS YOU WISH.

I GAVE MY WORD TO ABIDE BY THE COURT'S DECISION,

BUT, HOW CAN I MEEKLY *SUBMIT* TO MY FATE WHEN IT MAY CAUSE THE *EXTERMINATION* OF MUTANTKIND?!

AM I RATIONALIZING?

IS IT ONLY *DEATH* I REALLY FEAR?

NO! I CANNOT PERMIT THE SLAUGHTER OF MY PEOPLE!

I MUST BE STRONG, AND CONCENTRATE... *CONCENTRATE...*

AND, MERE MOMENTS LATER, HALF A WORLD AWAY...

BEHOLD--!

THE HOUR OF OUR VENGEANCE IS AT HAND!

EARLY THE NEXT MORNING...

...STATEMENTS WHICH MADE *DU MOTIER* SOUND LIKE A RACIST!

WE HAVE NO *PROOF* THAT HE ACTUALLY HOLDS THOSE OPINIONS, OR THAT HE LET THEM AFFECT HIS *JUDGMENT* IN THIS CASE.

SSH! MAGNETO JUST ENTERED THE COURTROOM.

THE FACES OF THE X-MEN GROW GRIM, TAUT.

THEY EXPECT THE WORST.

THEY ARE RARELY DISAPPOINTED.

HOWEVER, AT THAT PRECISE INSTANT--

--A FUSE BOX THREE FLOORS BELOW SUDDENLY CHOOSES TO MALFUNCTION...

FSSST

AND...

THE *LIGHTS*--!

OF ALL THE TIMES FOR A *BLACKOUT!*

IT WILL TAKE A FEW MINUTES BEFORE REPAIRS CAN BE MADE.

I WOULD PREFER TO SPEND THAT TIME IN SOLITUDE.

OF COURSE.

THIS *COULDN'T* BE MERE COINCIDENCE!

MAGNETO'S STALLING FOR TIME! *WHY?* WHAT'S HIS PLAN?

WE'LL BE RIGHT OUTSIDE!

THANK YOU.

CAN'T LET MY CONCENTRATION SLIP!

THE *STRAIN* IS INCREDIBLE, BUT *I CAN'T FAIL!* IT'S SO *CLOSE!* ONLY A FEW MILES MORE, AND--

KRASHH

THAT SOUNDED LIKE A WINDOW SHATTERING!

HEY! THE DOOR'S STUCK! IT WON'T OPEN!

BWAM BWAM

POUND ALL YOU WANT, *FOOLS!* I NEED ONLY A FEW MORE MOMENTS TO ADJUST THIS CIRCUITRY!

THERE!

WHAT'S *WRONG* WITH ME? WHY DO I HESITATE?!

I'M ONLY DOING WHAT *MUST* BE DONE!

"I REALLY DON'T HAVE ANY CHOICE!"

"I *NEVER* DID!"

≥UGN≤

CHIEF JUSTICE, ARE YOU *WELL?*

PLEASE FORGIVE ME.

I MUST NOW OBLITERATE THIS HELMET AND ITS CIRCUITRY SO THAT I CAN NEVER BE TEMPTED BY IT, AGAIN!

AND THEN...

THE DOOR-- IT SUDDENLY FLEW OPEN!

ARE YOU ALL RIGHT? WHAT HAPPENED TO THAT WINDOW?

WINDOW? WHAT WINDOW?

SHOULDN'T WE BE HEAD-ING BACK TO--

"--THE COURT-ROOM?"

THE SUBJECT OF THESE PROCEEDINGS IS THE THRESHOLD QUESTION. DOES THIS COURT HAVE JURISDICTION?

DOES IT HAVE THE RIGHT TO TRY THE ACCUSED FOR VIOLATING THE PROTOCOLS OF THE INTERNATIONAL LAWS OF WAR?

THAT QUESTION MUST BE ANSWERED LONG BEFORE THIS COURT CAN EVEN BEGIN TO JUDGE WHETHER OR NOT MAGNETO HAS EXCEEDED THE ACCEPTABLE BOUNDARIES OF FORCE ASSOCIATED WITH CONVENTIONAL WARFARE.

MAGNETO IS ACCUSED OF CRIMES AGAINST HUMANITY.

AFTER HEARING THE EVIDENCE PRESENTED HERE, THIS COURT RULES THAT THESE ALLEGED CRIMES WERE, IN FACT, COMMITTED DURING THAT PERIOD OF TIME WHEN MAGNETO WAS IN A STATE OF WAR AGAINST THE HUMAN RACE.

ONLY STATES OR THEIR EQUIVALENTS HAVE THE RIGHT TO DECLARE WAR.

THEREFORE, IN THIS COURTROOM, MAGNETO *MUST* BE ACCORDED THE SAME RIGHTS AND PRIVILEGES AS ANY OTHER WARRING STATE.

SINCE HE HAS NEVER SIGNED THE GENEVA CONVENTIONS, IT IS THE OPINION OF THIS COURT THAT IT HAS *NO JURISDICTION* OVER THE ACCUSED.

WHILE MAGNETO MAY HAVE VIOLATED THE LAWS OF CERTAIN INDIVIDUAL STATES AND NATIONS, AND MAY STILL BE LIABLE TO THEIR JUSTICE, THIS COURT HAS NO RIGHT TO JUDGE HIM.

HE IS FREE TO GO!

CONGRATULATIONS! YOU MADE IT!

YES...

WHY AREN'T THE OTHER JUDGES RAISING THEIR VOICES IN PROTEST OVER *DU MOTIER'S* SUDDEN CHANGE OF HEART?

OR, WAS I WRONG ABOUT HIM? IS THIS THE VERDICT HE HAD ALWAYS PLANNED FOR ME?

HOW CAN I EVER KNOW THE TRUTH?

BE CAREFUL! IT LOOKS LIKE THE START OF A RIOT OUTSIDE!

THE TRIAL WAS FIXED!

THAT MANIAC DESERVES DEATH!

WHY DIDN'T I ANTICIPATE THIS?

KEEP THAT FREAK OFF THE STREETS!

I WAS SO CONCERNED WITH THE EFFECTS MY DEATH WOULD HAVE ON MUTANTKIND--I NEVER ONCE CONSIDERED HOW MUCH MY FREEDOM WOULD *ENRAGE* MANKIND-- WOULD INCREASE THEIR *HATRED* AND *FEAR* OF US!

WILL THIS SET OFF THE WAR THAT I FEARED-- AND SOUND THE DEATH KNELL OF ALL MUTANTKIND?!

WHAT HAVE I DONE?

WHAT HAVE I DONE?!

DEATH TO MAGNETO

KILL THE FREAKS!

MEN NOT MUT